THE LEFTOVERS

USE THEIR HEADS!

Tristan Howard

A
LITTLE **APPLE**
PAPERBACK

SCHOLASTIC INC.
New York   Toronto   London   Auckland   Sydney

ISBN 0-590-89896-5

Produced by Daniel Weiss Associates, Inc.
33 West 17th Street, New York, NY 10011

12 11 10 9 8 7 6 5 4 3 2 1   6 7 8 9/9 0 1/0

Printed in the U.S.A.   40

First Scholastic printing, August 1996

Chapter 1

"Hey, Catherine! Want to see me score a goal?" Matt Carter asked. He picked up a soccer ball and bounced it on the ground.

I grinned. "Sure," I called back.

Matt looked at the ball. Then he looked at the goal. "Here I go!" he yelled.

"Hey, Matt!" I cried. "You forgot the ball!"

But Matt wasn't listening. As fast as he could, he ran between the goalposts and tumbled into the net at the back. "Goal!" he shouted.

1

"You're silly," I told him. But I couldn't help smiling.

Matt's best friend, Lucy Marcus, ran over to us, holding another ball. "Guess what?" she called out. "I can stand on my soccer ball without even falling off!"

"Show us," Matt said as he untangled himself from the net.

Lucy set her soccer ball down. Then she put her left foot on it. "It's a little tricky," she said, picking up her right foot—

The soccer ball **crash!** squirted away, and Lucy fell. "Ow!" she shouted.

"Are you all right?" Matt looked worried.

"I guess so." Lucy stood up slowly. Her eyes looked a little teary. "But I

2

really can do it. Where'd my ball go?"

"Kids!" I could hear my mother calling.

"Well, I'll show you later," Lucy said.

My name is Catherine Antler. I'm in third grade. Lucy, Matt, and I all play on a team called the Rangers. During the summer we're in a baseball league. But in the fall we play soccer.

I like the kids on my team, but there are two problems. One is that our team is made up of a bunch of leftovers—the kids no other team wanted. Some of my teammates are kind of crazy, and my best friends—Amy Powell and Michael Grassi—don't play with us. They're on the Orioles.

The other problem is that my mom is the coach. Mom doesn't know anything about baseball, but she had to coach because nobody else could.

Guess what? She doesn't know anything about soccer, either.

"Danny and Julie, please come out from behind those big poles," she was saying. Danny West and Julie Zimmer were playing follow-the-leader in one of the goals.

I groaned. "Mom, they're called goalposts," I said loudly.

Mom shrugged. "Poles, goalposts. It's the same thing."

I looked at Matt and Lucy and made a face.

"Who thinks they'll have fun playing soccer this fall?" Mom asked.

I saw Lucy's hand go shooting up. Quickly I raised my hand, too.

Josh Ramos threw his hand in the air. "I'm going to have a blast. I'm great at soccer."

Adam Fingerhut stood on tiptoe so his hand would be even higher than Josh's. "Oh, yeah?" he asked. "I'm great, too. I'm super great."

"Are you, Adam?" Mom smiled. She

turned to Alex Slavik. "How about you, Alex?"

Alex has feet that are way too big for him. He's not a very good baseball player. "I bet he'll be bad at soccer," I whispered to Matt. Matt grinned.

Alex twisted his toe into the grass. "I don't know, Mrs. Antler. I never played soccer before."

Mom patted his back. "That's okay, Alex. I'm sure you aren't the only one."

She was looking right at me. But I didn't say anything.

"I'm looking forward to soccer, too," Mitchell Rubin said in a robot voice. He was pretending to move like a robot, too, slowly and jerkily. "I like to play soccer a lot."

"Really?" Mom said. "Good for you!"

I was surprised. I like Mitchell. But in baseball he always falls asleep in the outfield. I couldn't imagine him being any good at soccer.

Matt nudged me. "Can you kick the ball while you're sleeping?" he whispered.

"All right," Mom said. "First we'll practice passing the ball. Find a partner, and we'll get started."

Matt and Lucy grabbed each other. I chose Yin Wong, who came to Maplewood from China. Mom gave Yin a soccer ball.

"Kick the ball to your partner," she told us. "When it gets to you, stop it with your foot." She put her foot on top of the ball to show us.

"Hey, I can do that," Lucy said happily. "I can even stand on it. Want to see?"

Mom blew her whistle. "Go!"

"Soccer's really hard," Yin muttered. She pulled her foot way back. Then she kicked as hard as she could.

She missed.

"Soccer's way too hard!" Yin glared at the ball.

"Kick with a little less force," Mom suggested.

Yin tried again. This time she kicked it! But the ball rolled only two feet.

"Good try, Yin," I said. "Kick it again."

Yin shook her head. She reached down and picked up the ball.

"You can't do that, Yin!" I shouted. "In soccer you aren't supposed to touch the ball with your hands!"

"You can't use your hands?" Yin asked. "What a dumb game!" She rolled the ball across the ground. I put out my foot to stop it. But I was too late. The ball was already past me.

When I caught up to it, I tried to kick it back to Yin. But it rolled off to the side instead. "Sorry!" I yelled as Yin ran after it.

At least it was a good hard kick.

I looked around while I waited for Yin to bring the ball back. Other kids were having trouble, too.

I saw Matt trying to pass to Lucy. *Wham!* His foot hit the grass first. A chunk of dirt and grass flew up from the ground. The ball rolled about three inches.

"Try again, Matt!" Mom yelled.

Matt stuck out his lip and kicked the grass again. This time the ball didn't even move.

I looked at Adam and Josh. "Come on, Adam!" Josh was shouting. "Just stop the stupid ball!"

"Well, you're kicking it too hard!" Adam yelled back. He gave the ball a gigantic kick—and fell right on his bottom.

Next I watched Alex. He was standing on one foot with his tongue sticking out. Slowly he brought his other foot toward the ball. But when his toe hit it, the ball barely moved.

"Harder, Alex," Mom said.

"Catherine!" Yin threw our ball at me from a long way away. Quickly I pressed my knees together and hoped it would hit my shin guards.

But the ball bounced off to the side.

"Hey, Catherine!" Mitchell was yelling at me as I chased my ball. "Watch this!"

He bent his leg way back and kicked hard. The ball went sailing through the air. But so did his shoe. In fact, the shoe went farther than the ball.

Mitchell turned red. "Oops," he said.

I laughed. "I think your shoes are too big."

Mitchell picked up his shoe. "I guess I should tie my shoes really tight," he said slowly. He looked at the shoe and

wiggled his toes. "Well, anyway, now I know why they call this game soccer."

"You do?" I couldn't help frowning. "Why?"

Mitchell wiggled his toes again and pointed to his foot. "Get it?"

"Get what?" I looked down at his foot. Mitchell's shoe was still off, and he was only wearing—

His sock.

"Sock-er!" I hit myself on the head and grinned. "Now I get it!"

Mitchell smiled.

We practiced passing for ten minutes. Yin and I hardly made a single pass that worked. Sometimes I didn't kick the ball right. Sometimes Yin didn't kick it right. And sometimes we couldn't stop the ball when it got to us.

At last Mom blew her whistle. "Come on over," she told us.

Matt dropped onto his knees. "Look!" he shouted. "My feet are gone!"

Lucy dropped onto her knees, too. "It's easier this way," she said, trying to kick the ball with her thigh.

Mom blew her whistle for quiet. "How many people found that passing was hard?" she asked.

Yin and I raised our hands. So did Alex.

"Lucy? Matt?" Mom asked.

They raised their hands, too. "Why are we raising our hands?" I heard Matt whisper to Lucy.

"Adam's hand should be up," Josh said loudly. "Adam can't play soccer."

"I can so!" Adam balled his hands into fists. "I'm really good at soccer. I'm better than you any day."

"No, you're not," Josh said with a snort.

"Let's let Adam decide, Josh," Mom said. "Did you think passing was hard, Adam?"

"No way," Adam grunted. He sat on his hands, in case they might go up by themselves.

Mom nodded. "Fine," she said. "I'd

like you to make two lines. We'll practice passing from one line to the other." She divided us into two groups.

"Everybody on my team line up behind me," Josh said. We all got into line behind Josh. I tried to get in second, but Danny pushed in front of me.

"Ow!" Matt said. "Stop pushing, Yin! That really hurts!"

Someone knocked into me from behind. I bumped against Danny. "Hey!" he said, turning around and giving me a push, too. "Quit shoving, Catherine!"

"No, you quit shoving!" I gave Danny a little push back.

"I'm not pushing you." Danny glared at me. "Josh is the one who's pushing."

"You don't have to get so close to me," Josh said. He bounced up and down, ready to kick.

"Don't kick it too hard, Josh," said Julie. She was at the front of the other line. "These are new sweatpants, and I don't want to get them dirty." Julie cares a lot about how she looks.

"Ready?" Josh demanded.

Julie looked around and put her hands on her hips. "No pushing back there."

"I'm not pushing," Alex said sadly. "It's Mitchell who—"

"Here I go!" Josh yelled. He pulled his foot back and kicked hard. The ball sailed right at Julie. **Wham!**

Julie was just turning back to face Adam. Her eyes got very big when she saw the ball coming. "Help!" she cried. But it was too late.

"Oof!" The ball hit her right in the stomach. Julie waved her arms to try to keep her balance. She staggered back—and bumped into Alex.

"Watch out!" Alex yelled. He fell backward, too. One moment I could see his head. The next moment I couldn't.

"Stop pushing!" Lucy yelled, just as

15

Alex landed on top of her. She reached out to steady herself against Mitchell.

"Hey!" shouted Mitchell. He leaned backward and—

Boom. Boom. Boom.

I rubbed my eyes. Everyone in the other line was lying on the ground, knocked over. Just like a row of dominoes! My line started to laugh.

"If that was bowling, I'd have gotten a strike," Josh joked as Mom helped the other kids up. I saw that Mitchell's shoe had fallen off again.

Mom took a deep breath. "Let's talk about how to play soccer," she said.

"I already know how to play soccer." Lucy sat down on the ground and started to whistle. She plucked a handful of grass and let it trickle down onto her leg.

Mom wasn't listening. "First there's the goalie," she said. "Anyone know what the goalie does?"

Mitchell lay down on the grass. "The

17

goalie stops the ball from going into the goal," he said in his robot voice.

"That's right!" Mom said. "Now—"

"Mrs. Antler?" Alex tugged on Mom's sleeve. "I thought you were *supposed* to get the ball into the goal in soccer."

"You are," Mitchell explained. "The goalie stops the *other* team from getting a goal." He thought for a moment. "It's like in outer space."

"It's like *what*?" Mom asked.

"Like in outer space," Mitchell repeated. "If you stood in outer space and you were really big, you could kick the earth. The earth is like a gigantic soccer ball. And the goalie would have to keep it out of the sun."

"Oh." Alex nodded. "I get it."

"How come you know so much about outer space?" Danny wanted to know. He poked Mitchell.

Mitchell smiled. "Because sometimes

aliens from outer space send me messages through my shoes." He held the shoe to his ear like a telephone. "See?"

"Do the aliens make your shoes fall off, too?" I asked curiously.

"Maybe." He listened very hard to his shoe. "Right now the aliens are thinking of words that rhyme with goalie. Boalie, moalie, joalie—"

"Thank you, Mitchell," Mom said quickly. "Everybody else plays either offense or defense."

"Where's the fence?" Alex asked, looking around.

"Yeah, what fence?" Matt asked, throwing a handful of grass in the air.

"Off-fence," Julie said. She rolled her eyes. "De-fence. There aren't any fences, Alex. It's just the words."

"That's right." Mom nodded. "*Offense* means when you are trying to score the goals. *Defense* means—"

"When you're trying to keep the

other guys from scoring," Mitchell said.

"Very good, Mitchell," Mom said.

Mitchell gave her a shy grin. "The aliens told me," he said, tapping his shoe.

I was impressed that my mom knew all this stuff about soccer. Then I saw that she had a little piece of paper in her hand. Suddenly I understood.

She had all that information written down.

She was cheating!

Chapter 3

"Josh and Mitchell, show us how to pass," Mom said a few minutes later. Next to me, Matt pretended to snore, and Lucy was still dropping grass on her legs.

Mitchell got to his feet and slipped his shoe back on. "Me?" He sounded pleased.

"Mitchell?" Danny frowned. Danny was wearing fancy shin guards, elbow pads, and a headband that said "Kick It!" in bright blue letters. He has more

sports equipment than anybody I know. "But Mrs. Antler, Mitchell isn't—"

Danny stopped. I knew what he was going to say, though: that Mitchell wasn't any good.

"Watch," Mom said. She set the ball on the ground. "Ready, Mitchell?"

Mitchell tried to hide a grin. He pulled one foot back and kicked.

The ball rose into the air, bounced, and rolled right to where Josh was standing.

So did Mitchell's shoe.

"Wow!" Lucy poked Matt. "That was a pretty good kick, huh?" She pulled up some more grass and dropped it on Matt's lap.

"Wow yourself." Matt poked her

right back and threw the grass onto her legs.

"Here," Josh said. He picked up Mitchell's shoe and threw it back to him.

"I guess that's why they call it of-fense," Mitchell said with a little smile as he put his shoe back on.

"What do you mean?" Julie asked.

"My shoe came *off*," Mitchell explained shyly. "So that's why they call it *off*-fense. An alien told me that one," he explained.

"Good kick, Mitchell," Mom said. "Did you all see how Mitchell hit the ball with the inside of his foot? Now it's Josh's turn."

Josh took a running start. "I'm going to boot it across the field!" he boasted.

"Not too hard, Josh!" Mom warned him. But Josh had kicked the ball already. I gasped as it zoomed into the air. It seemed as if it would never come down.

"What did I tell you!" Josh looked

proudly at the ball flying over Mitchell's head.

"I don't think I can stop it with my foot, Mrs. Antler," Mitchell said unhappily.

Mom rolled Josh another ball. "Gently," she told him. "Kick it on the ground."

"That's boring," Josh complained.

"He'll kick it hard again," Yin predicted.

Wham! Yin was right. And the ball was heading right for Mitchell's head!

But Mitchell didn't duck. Instead he jumped toward the ball. I couldn't believe it. "Mitchell!" I screamed.

Mitchell jerked his head forward. There

was a thud. The ball bounced off his forehead and rolled right back to Josh.

For a moment no one said a word.

"Did you do that on purpose?" Alex said at last. His eyes were so big, I thought they might pop out of his head.

"Did aliens teach you how?" Danny asked.

"I wish I could do that," Matt said.

"Mitchell, are you all right?" Lucy asked. She was still pulling up grass. Her legs were completely green.

Mitchell just grinned. "Pretty neat play, huh?" He tapped his head. "I practice that a lot at my house."

"Very nice, Mitchell," Mom said. I could tell she was impressed. "Josh, next time do it more gently." Then she turned to the rest of us. "Anyone want to take Josh's place?"

"Well, I can still kick it harder than anybody," Josh muttered as he sat down.

A few kids waved their hands, but I didn't. I didn't want anybody to see that I couldn't kick very well. Mom looked around. "Okay, Brenda," she said.

"All *right*!" Brenda yelled. She pumped her fist in the air. "I won't kick it too hard, Mrs. Antler," she promised.

Brenda? I'd forgotten about Brenda Bailey. She was probably our worst baseball player. She was nice, and she could get very excited about things. But she sure couldn't catch.

Matt leaned close to me. "This will be funny."

"That's because she won't kick it at all," I whispered back to Matt. I pictured Brenda trying to pass the ball. She'd be worse than me for sure, I thought. Worse than Matt and Lucy. Worse than Alex.

Well, maybe not worse than Alex.

"I bet she falls down," Lucy said.

Aiming carefully, Brenda kicked—

And the ball rolled straight to Mitchell.

Brenda's face broke into the biggest, widest grin I'd ever seen. She gave a squeal and jumped up and down.

Matt poked me. "Did you see that?" he said in amazement.

I stared at Brenda. "Uh-huh," I whispered. "But I bet she can't do it again."

Mitchell stopped the ball with his foot, just like a real soccer player. Then he kicked it back.

And Brenda stopped it, too! Her foot moved fast—fast as lightning.

"How am I doing, Mrs. Antler?" Brenda asked.

"Very nice, Brenda," Mom said, smiling.

I looked over at Matt and Lucy. For once Matt was paying attention. And Lucy had even stopped pulling up grass.

Brenda turned her foot so the side of her shoe faced the ball. Then she swung her leg forward. *Smack!* The ball rolled back to Mitchell.

"Yes!" shouted Brenda. She clapped her hands and pumped her fist.

I stared at Matt and Lucy. They stared back at me.

"She's pretty good," Lucy said, biting her lip.

"She is," Matt agreed. "Both of them are."

"And they're so bad at baseball," I added with a frown. "We're way better at baseball than they are—"

I stopped in the middle of my sentence. But Matt finished it for me.

"But they're better at soccer," he said sadly.

Chapter

"How's soccer going, Catherine?" my best friend Amy asked on Friday. We were in the cafeteria at school.

"All right, I guess." I shrugged. I didn't really want to talk about soccer. I took a bite of spaghetti and made a face. "This tastes awful. Don't you wish it was pizza day again?"

Amy laughed. "I wish every day was pizza day."

"Me too," I said with a grin.

"Did you do thread-the-needle at

practice yesterday?" Amy asked.

"Thread-the-needle?" I stared at Amy.

"You know." Amy took another bite. "When you dribble the ball through an obstacle course. We did it yesterday. It was fun."

I frowned. "You don't dribble the ball in soccer," I said. "You only dribble in basketball."

"Not dribble with your hands," Amy said. "When you kick it just a little way with each kick, that's soccer dribbling."

"When you kick it," I repeated. "Oh, yeah, I knew that."

"Hi, Catherine." Michael, my other best friend, sat down next to us. "How's soccer?"

"Fine," I said quickly. "Did you do your math homework?"

But Michael wasn't listening. "Hey, Catherine," he asked, "did your soccer team do thread-the-needle yesterday at practice?"

I felt I had to answer the question this time. But I didn't want to tell Michael and Amy that I could barely even kick the ball. So I crossed my fingers behind my back. "Um—yeah," I said slowly.

Michael grinned. "Isn't it neat?" he asked. "Our team is really good at it."

"We're going to play you guys on Tuesday," Amy said. "I can't wait!"

I choked on my milk.

"Neither can I," I said when I was done choking.

After school Mom drove us to the soccer field. Matt and Lucy were already there, trying to stand on their soccer balls.

"Hi, Catherine!" Matt yelled. "Watch!"

He stepped on his ball. It flew out from under him. Matt landed on the ground with a thud. "Well, I almost had it," he said.

"This is how," Lucy told him. She

balanced against a tree trunk and climbed onto the ball. Then she let go and—

Whoosh! The ball squirted away. Lucy fell against the tree.

"Maybe I'll show you tomorrow," she said.

When everyone arrived, Mom got us together. "First let's practice some more passes," she said.

"No fair!" Josh said. "Let's try to kick it into the goal from the other end of the field."

"No, let's play a practice game," said Danny. He had a new headband on that day. It was neon green, and it said "Gooooal!" in black letters.

Mom smiled. "Later, Danny. Josh, in

soccer you have to work together, and that means passing—and sharing the ball."

Josh made a face. "No fair," he said again.

I raised my hand. "Mom," I said, "can't we do thread-the-needle instead?"

Mom frowned. "Thread-the-what?"

"Thread-the-needle," I said. "You make a big obstacle course, and you have to kick the ball through it."

Brenda spoke up. "You zigzag, Mrs. Antler. You dribble the ball around the goalposts and stuff. It's fun." She smiled that big smile again.

"Can you do it on your knees?" Matt asked. He was trying to balance a ball on his head, but it kept falling off.

Mom shook her head. "Not today, Catherine. I don't think we're ready for thread-the-needle yet." Then she grinned. "Except maybe a couple of us."

Brenda and Mitchell grinned back.

But Matt, Lucy, and I didn't.

Chapter

5

"Okay, guys," Mom said after we finished passing. "We're going to play a practice game." She pointed to all the kids on my side of her. "This is the red team: Catherine, Matt, Lucy, Josh, Adam, and Yin."

"Slaughter team!" Josh announced. "We're going to rule!"

I looked around. The red team was a pretty good baseball team, I thought.

But I wasn't so sure we would be good at soccer.

"The blue team," Mom went on, "is Mitchell, Julie, Alex, Danny, and Brenda."

Danny pulled at Mom's sweater. "That's not fair, Mrs. Antler," he said. "They have six players, and we only have five."

Mom smiled. "I think it will be all right, Danny," she said. Then she told the blue team to go to the other side of the field.

"I'm captain of the red team," Josh said. "If you get the ball, pass it to me."

"No way!" Adam said loudly. "Who said you could be captain anyway?"

"Because I'm the best player," Josh said even more loudly.

Lucy turned a cartwheel. "Can anybody else do this?" she asked.

"Can anybody else do *this*?" Matt asked. He squatted and pulled his shirt over his shin guards. "I'm a frog!" he croaked. "Ribbit, ribbit, ribbit!"

"You're a pretty dumb frog," Adam said.

"You're just mad because Josh is a better player than you are," Lucy said.

"Red team!" Suddenly I realized Mom was yelling to us. "You need a goalie!"

"What's a goalie?" Matt asked in a silly voice. He fell over backward. "Ribbit, ribbit, splat!" he croaked.

"It's the person who keeps the ball out of the goal," I reminded him. "The only one who can use his hands."

"Hands?" Yin smiled. "I'll play goalie," she said, wiggling her fingers.

The rest of us went to the middle of the field. A soccer field looks like a big box. It has four white lines and a goal at each end. If you kick the ball outside the lines, the other team gets to throw it back in.

Throw  In

Mom put the ball down in front of Mitchell. "The first kick of the game is called the kickoff," she said, checking her card.

"It probably will be," Mitchell said. He smiled his shy smile. "I'll probably kick off my shoe."

"Tie it tightly," Mom suggested. "Ready? Go!"

Mitchell kicked off to Brenda. He was right—his shoe did come off. It soared through the air and landed almost on top of Brenda's head. Brenda dribbled forward. With the ball, I mean, not the shoe. Then she passed it back.

"Get the ball, red team!" Mom yelled.

I tried. I ran toward Mitchell. But the next thing I knew, Mitchell was way in front of me. Even with only one shoe on!

"Nice dribbling, Mitchell!" Mom

cried. "Come on, red team! Get the ball!"

Josh and Adam ran forward. Adam ducked at the last minute. Josh stuck out his foot. But Mitchell saw him coming. He passed back to Brenda.

Brenda kicked it forward. Then she kicked it again—and again. It looked as if the ball was tied to her leg with an invisible string.

The only people left between her and the goal were Yin and Matt—and Matt was pretending to be a frog again!

"Matt!" I yelled. But Matt wasn't even looking at Brenda. Yin tried to block the ball, but it was no use. Brenda kicked it right into the net.

GOOOO

"*Gooooal!*" bellowed Brenda in the loudest voice I'd ever heard. The blue team cheered. Brenda pumped her fist and grinned.

"You should have stopped that ball," Josh told Adam. "Are you chicken or something?"

"Good passes, blue team," Mom said. "Matt, remember to stand up, dear."

"Do we get the ball now?" Lucy asked. "I want to kick off."

We all went back to the middle of the field. I picked up Mitchell's shoe and gave it back to him. But first I put it up to my ear and listened hard.

It was funny—I couldn't hear a thing.

"Stand right here, Lucy," Mom said. "All right. Red team—go!"

Lucy kicked the ball as hard as she

AAAALL!

could. It rolled very slowly to Julie. Julie stopped it with her foot and kicked it back.

"Lucy!" I yelled. "Get the ball!"

Lucy watched it roll right past her. She looked just like a statue. I'd never seen her stand so still.

"Time out!" Mom squatted next to Lucy. "Why didn't you kick it again?"

"The ball was there." Lucy pointed. "You told me to stand right here."

"Oh." Mom nodded. "In soccer you have to go *to* the ball," she said gently.

Lucy made a face. "In baseball the ball comes to you."

"I know," Mom said. "But this is different. Catherine, want to try it?"

"Sure!" I said. I pulled my foot way back. I thought I'd blast the ball to the other side of the world, but instead it rolled toward Alex. At least my shoe stayed on.

"Get it, Alex!" Mom shouted.

Alex stared at the ball coming toward him. Slowly he swung his right leg back.

"Kick it hard!" Mitchell yelled.

Alex pulled his leg back even farther. The ball hit his left leg instead. "Oof!" Alex cried, falling to the ground.

"Alex!" Danny sounded exasperated. "If you can't kick it, get out of the way!"

Josh ran up. "Look out!" he shouted. He kicked the ball as hard as he could. It sailed toward the goal—and way over it.

At least *ten feet* over it.

"Wow!" Josh said as he watched it go.

"Too high, Josh!" Mom called out. "Pass next time. Or dribble until you're closer to the goal."

"Dribble?" said Matt in a silly voice. "Did someone say dribble?" I could see him pretending to drool, just like a little baby.

"Not that kind of dribble," Mom said. She handed Julie another ball.

Julie kicked it to Mitchell. Mitchell kicked it high into the air. "Use your head!" I could hear him shout.

Three people jumped for the ball: Danny and Brenda from the blue team, and Josh from ours.

"Look out!" Mom blew her whistle.

The ball bounced off Brenda's head. An instant later there was a huge crash. Brenda, Josh, and Danny all collided in midair!

"It was my ball," Josh said angrily. "You're supposed to get out of the way."

Danny pressed his hands tightly against his ears. "Feel my head and see if it's broken!" he gasped.

"You're okay," Brenda told him. She stood up and grinned. "You guys have hard heads! But you have to go for the ball, not the other player."

Mom picked up the ball. "Matt, it's your turn to kick off."

Matt squatted down and panted. "No, thanks, Mrs. Antler. I'm too hot."

"Too hot?" Mom looked surprised.

"From all that running," Matt explained. He fanned himself with his hand.

"I'm tired, too," Lucy said. She shut her eyes and lay down next to Matt. "Wake me up at the end of the game," she said.

"Can we keep playing, Mrs. Antler?" Mitchell asked hopefully. "I didn't get a goal yet."

"I like baseball better," Matt said from the grass. "In baseball you don't have to run so much."

"I like baseball better, too," Lucy agreed. "In baseball people don't keep the ball away from you."

"Baseball lets you use your hands," Yin said.

Mom sighed. "But we're playing soccer now," she reminded us. "Come on, Adam. You can kick off."

It was lucky we weren't keeping score. The red team would have lost by about a hundred points. Every time we got the ball, Josh would try to kick it into the goal, no matter where he was. He never made it. Not even once.

We didn't get the ball very much, though. Mitchell and Brenda kept passing it where we couldn't get it. They scored lots of goals. Julie and Danny scored, too. The only player on the blue team who didn't score was Alex.

I didn't get a goal. Neither did Matt or Lucy.

We didn't even come close.

Chapter 6

It was Monday afternoon. We were about to start practice again. But some of us weren't very happy to be there.

"I'd rather be playing baseball." Matt sighed. He sat on his soccer ball and pretended to swing a bat. "Pow! I'd hit it out of the park."

"Yeah," Yin said. "Pow!" She swung a pretend bat, too.

"Baseball is more fun," Lucy agreed. "Don't you think so, Catherine?"

I nodded. I'd practiced soccer a lot

over the weekend, but the ball still wouldn't go where I tried to kick it. Suddenly I had an idea. "Hey!" I said. "Let's play baseball right now!"

"Yeah!" Matt got off his soccer ball. "I'm pitcher. Ready?"

I picked up a long stick to use as a bat. Matt tossed me the soccer ball. I swung. *Wham!* The stick broke. The ball bounced away. Lucy went to field it, and I ran over to a tree. "Safe at first!" I yelled.

Mitchell dribbled over to us. "What are you guys doing?"

"Playing baseball," Yin told him with a frown. "It's a good game. You can use your hands."

"Soccer's a great game," Mitchell told us. "I love to play soccer."

"How come?" I asked. I was curious. "We like baseball better."

Mitchell shrugged. "I like soccer best. You get to run around a lot. In baseball all you do is stand there. It's kind of boring."

"Is that why you fall asleep in the outfield all the time?" Matt wanted to know.

Mitchell grinned. "Sometimes I just rest," he said. "But I do like to run around. I like games where you can do that." He paused. "Anyway," he added, "I don't think they play baseball on the planet Neptune."

He tossed the ball up and let it bounce off his head. Then he caught it again.

"That's pretty neat," I said. "I wish I could do that, too."

"Well, I don't," Lucy said before Mitchell could speak. "I still think soccer's a pretty dumb game." She held out the ball. "Come on, guys. Batter up!"

"Hey, kids!" It was Mom calling.

Lucy wrinkled her nose. "We'll finish our game later," she said, and we walked over to start practice.

"Our first game is tomorrow," Mom reminded us. "So we have a lot to work on today."

Danny raised his hand. That day his headband was blue and gold, and it had little pictures of soccer balls on it. "Can we practice using our heads?" he asked.

Mom laughed. "I hope all of you will use your heads all the time!" she said.

"That isn't what I mean," Danny said. "Can we bonk the ball with our heads, the way Brenda and Mitchell did?"

"Not me," Julie said. She patted her head. "I just washed my hair this morning."

"Yeah, come on, Mrs. Antler," Josh said. He stood up. "I bet I can head the ball into the goal from here!"

"All right," Mom said. "If you'd like a turn, line up behind Mitchell."

Brenda stood up. So did Josh and Adam. After a moment Matt and I got at the end of the line. It looked a little scary, but it also looked kind of fun.

"Lucy?" Mom asked.

"No, thanks, Mrs. Antler." Lucy did a somersault. "Soccer's not very interesting. I'd rather do somersaults."

"All right." Mom tossed the ball to Mitchell. He ducked to hit it with his head and made it bounce right back to her hands. It looked easy.

"I bet I can do that," I whispered to Matt.

Brenda was next. She hit it right back to Mom off the side of her head. "Yeah!" she shouted happily. I had to laugh. It was amazing how loud a small person like Brenda could be.

"Nice job, Brenda!" Mom said.

Matt and I looked over at Lucy. She was trying to balance on her soccer ball again. As we watched she slipped off. The ball rolled away.

Matt poked me. "When the ball comes to us, maybe we should try standing on it instead of kicking it," he suggested.

I grinned. "Yeah. Then maybe it would go somewhere."

"Too hard, Josh!" Mom said. I turned around. Josh had headed the ball hard, all right. But he hadn't gotten it anywhere near Mom.

"I really whacked it," Josh said happily.

Next it was Adam's turn. I thought he looked kind of nervous. "Duck your head a little when it comes," Mom said. She tossed the ball.

Adam ducked. Then he ducked some more—and some more. At the last moment he dropped onto the ground and covered his head with his hands. The ball hit his elbow and bounced away.

"Chicken!" Josh said.

"I am not!" Adam frowned. "I just couldn't see it, that's all."

"Would you like to try again, Adam?" Mom asked gently. She picked up the ball.

Adam thought about it. "Um—no. Not right now."

Danny headed the ball pretty well. When it was Alex's turn, he tripped when he was trying to duck. He fell down and decided not to try again.

Then it was Matt's turn. He squatted, wiggled his legs up into his shirt again, and pretended to be a frog.

"Can't you stand up, Matt?" Mom asked.

"I like doing it this way," Matt told her.

Mom shrugged and threw the ball. Matt sat perfectly still. It bounced off the top of his head and rolled behind him.

Mom sighed and got a new ball.

Matt waddled back to Lucy. "I bet I could stand on the soccer ball like this," he said.

"Ready, Catherine?" Mom asked.

I swallowed hard. Suddenly the ball seemed very big. And very heavy. "Um—I think so," I said.

Mom tossed the ball in the air. I tried to guess where it would come down. First I moved back. Then I moved forward.

"Get it, Catherine!" Mitchell shouted.

I blinked. It looked as if the ball was coming at a million miles an hour! I thought about screaming. But instead I slid onto the ground. The ball landed behind me with a thud.

"Do you want to try again?" Mom said.

I shook my head. "Not right now." And maybe not ever, I thought. Trying to hit the ball with your head was pretty scary!

I sighed. Soccer really was too hard.

And how could you have fun playing a game if you weren't very good at it?

Chapter 7

On Tuesday we had our game against
the Orioles.

It looked as though it was going to
be a slaughter.

I watched the Orioles coach kick
soccer balls to them. They all stopped
the passes with their feet, and then
they kicked the balls into the net.
Boom. Boom. Boom. They hardly ever
missed.

"We couldn't do that," I said. I
thought of the day when half of our

team had fallen over like dominoes. *Boom. Boom. Boom.*

Lucy shrugged. "You're probably right." She put her ball on the ground. "Want to see me stand on it? I'm getting lots better."

The referee blew her whistle. It was time for the game to begin.

Mom gave us all an encouraging smile. "Go, Rangers!" she said.

"Go, Rangers!" we all said. But some of us didn't say it as if we meant it. I made a face. I wished we were playing baseball instead.

The Orioles kicked off. Michael dribbled past Lucy and Yin. Alex fell down. Then Michael passed to another Oriole, who kicked it right by Danny, the goalie. The game was only one minute old, and already we were losing.

On the kickoff, Adam tried to pass to Julie, but he didn't kick very hard. One of the Orioles stole the ball.

"Come on, defense!" Mom yelled.

Yin ran forward. She picked up the ball and threw it.

Tweet! The referee blew her whistle again.

"Hand ball," Mitchell said. He put his hands behind his back to show Yin. "Don't use your hands."

"Boy, that's dumb," Yin said, and glared at Mitchell.

The Orioles got a free kick. A minute later they scored again.

AAAALL!

"I'm tired," Lucy said to Mom. "Can I have a rest now?" In soccer, not everybody plays at once.

"In a minute," Mom said. "Come on, offense!"

This time I got to kick off. I kicked it pretty hard, but it went out of bounds, so the Orioles got it again.

Michael passed to Amy. Amy dribbled toward Lucy—

But Lucy was on her back with her eyes closed, pretending to snore!

"Lucy!" Mom yelled. Lucy didn't get up. Danny tried to get the ball, but Amy kicked it past him. 3–0.

We got a little better after that. Mitchell scored a goal. So did Brenda. Josh had a couple of good hard kicks. But it was 7–2 at halftime. And Mitchell had lost his shoe more times than we had scored goals.

"This is too hard," I complained, drinking from my water bottle.

Matt took a drink, too. "I'll score lots of goals in the second half," he promised. "I'll dribble into the net. Get it? Dribble?" He let water trickle down his chin.

"We get it," said Julie. "But we don't want to get it."

"It's all Adam's fault," Josh said. "He always runs away from the ball."

"I do not!" Adam looked as if he might cry.

"It's okay to be worried about getting hit by the ball," Mom said. "Some of you feel that way when you play baseball, too."

"Not me," I said.

"Not me, either," Lucy said.

"Not me, either either," Matt said. He dribbled some more water out of his mouth.

"Some of you worry when you play baseball," Mom went on, "and some of you worry when you play soccer. It's okay."

"I worry all the time," Alex said sadly.

"I really like to use my feet," Brenda said, looking happy. Then she frowned. Suddenly she looked like the old Brenda—the one who couldn't play baseball very well. "But catching a ball is hard."

The second half started, and Mom sent other kids in to replace Matt, Lucy, and me. I was still thinking about what Mom had said. "Who are the best baseball players on our team?" I asked.

"Us," Lucy said.

"And Josh. And Yin." Matt ticked them off on his fingers. "And Adam."

"And who are the best soccer players?" I asked.

"Mitchell," Lucy said right away.

"And Brenda," Matt added.

"Danny and Julie are pretty good, too," I went on.

"And Josh," Matt said. "Don't forget Josh."

"Josh kicks the ball too hard," I said. "The best soccer players are the worst baseball players. Isn't that weird?"

"Come on, defense!" Mom yelled. We looked out at the field, where Alex was running for the ball. But he tripped over it and fell down.

"Well, there's Alex," I said. "He doesn't seem to be too good at either baseball or soccer."

Lucy nodded. "Yeah. At least Alex is worse at soccer than us."

There was a loud cheer. The Orioles had scored again.

Matt poked me. "Look out," he whispered. "Here comes Too Tall."

David "Too Tall" Henry is the biggest kid in the third grade. He's on the Orioles, and he's a great baseball player. He's also not a very nice kid.

"Uh-oh," Lucy said.

"I bet he's *good*," Matt said. "I bet he can really kick the ball."

I let out a huge sigh. I could imagine Too Tall scoring a goal from all the way across the field.

"Lucy! Matt! Catherine!" Mom yelled. "You're back in the game now."

"Uh-oh," Lucy said again. She looked at Too Tall and bit her lip.

"Double uh-oh," Matt said. "We'll *never* get the ball past him!"

"Come on, guys!" Mom yelled. "Let's go! Run!"

We walked.

Chapter 8

Too Tall looked bigger than ever. I hoped no one would kick the ball to me when I was near him.

"Ready?" The referee blew her whistle.

Julie kicked the ball hard, but Amy blocked it. Another Oriole kicked it toward our goal. She dribbled past Josh. Then she dribbled around Mitchell.

Only Alex was between her and the goalie.

"Come on, Alex!" Mom shouted.

"Another goal," Matt said softly. "Hey, Lucy! Let's look for caterpillars."

Alex ran forward. The Oriole player pulled her leg back to kick. *Wham!* The ball soared up toward the goal. Just then Alex tripped over his feet and fell.

I groaned. I thought it would be a goal for sure.

But the ball hit Alex's head and bounced away!

"That's using your head!" Mitchell shouted, running after the ball.

Alex struggled to his feet. He had a big grin on his face.

"*Yes!* What a play!" Brenda shouted. She sounded just like a real sports announcer. She slapped Alex five.

I gulped. The ball was rolling right to me!

"Step on it!" Mitchell shouted. I put out my foot the way I'd practiced with Yin. It worked! The ball stopped rolling. I took a deep breath. Then I kicked it forward.

"Go after it, Catherine!" Mom yelled. "Dribble!"

I blinked. The ball was rolling toward the Orioles' end of the field. I ran two steps forward and kicked it. I took another step and kicked it again. It kept rolling! It was kind of fun.

Then I looked up—and saw Too Tall in front of me.

"Help!" I screamed. I decided I'd better let him have the ball. I was ready to dive out of the way. But then I noticed something strange.

Too Tall was backing away.

I couldn't believe my eyes. I stuck

out my foot and kicked the ball as hard as I could.

And Too Tall ducked!

The goalie caught the ball before it went into the net, but I didn't care.

Mitchell caught up with me and grinned. "Nice breakaway, Catherine!"

"Thanks," I said. As I headed back across the field, I looked over at Too Tall. He looked a little scared.

"That was really good, Catherine!" Lucy told me. Her eyes were wide. "You were brave to run at Too Tall like that."

When the whistle blew at the end of the game, we shook hands with the Orioles. We'd lost by a lot. But I'd had fun—more fun than I'd thought I would have.

And if Too Tall Henry wasn't good at soccer, maybe it was okay that I wasn't very good, either.

"Nice game, Catherine." Michael

slapped my hand. "Nice game, Lucy."

"Nice game, Michael," Lucy said in a silly voice.

Michael laughed. "You played hard, Lucy," he said. "Remember when you almost scored a goal?"

"Oh, yeah." Lucy grinned. She had dribbled a ball past Too Tall, too. "That was fun. But I still like baseball better."

We had Popsicles after the game. Brenda ate three. Then we kicked the ball around a little.

"The next game is tomorrow," Mom told us. "You played well today, guys. I bet you'll be even better next time."

"I can score a goal," Matt told her. "See?" He dashed into the net. "Goal!" he shouted.

Mom smiled. "Maybe tomorrow you'll score a real goal, Matt."

Brenda showed Yin how to kick the ball with the inside of her foot. Finally

Yin kicked one into the net. "Goal!" she shouted. She pumped her fist just the way Brenda did. "Maybe soccer's not so dumb after all."

"It helps to practice," Mitchell said, taking off his shoe. "Adam, do you want to try heading the ball again?" He held the shoe up to his ear and listened. "The aliens say it might work this time."

"It'll probably break his head," Josh teased.

Adam stuck out his tongue at Josh. It was purple from the Popsicle. "Okay, I'll try."

Mitchell tossed him the ball. Adam held his breath, lunged—and hit it. Not very hard, but he hit it.

"Good job!" Mitchell called.

Adam grinned and stuck out his tongue at Josh again. Josh grinned, too, and stuck out his own tongue. It was orange.

"How about you, Catherine?" Mitchell asked.

I thought about saying yes. Then I remembered how big the ball had looked when it was coming at me. "Um—not yet, thanks," I said at last. "I don't think I'm ready."

I liked the way Brenda and Mitchell were trying to help the rest of us. I tried to remember if I'd helped them at baseball.

I didn't think I ever had.

Chapter 9

"I think you guys will play well today," Mom told me on the way to the game. She parked the car next to the field. It was Wednesday, and we were going to play the Pirates.

"I think so, too," I said. And I meant it. But I was thinking about something else as well. "Will I ever be as good at soccer as Mitchell?" I asked.

"If you work hard, you'll get better." Mom picked up the bag of soccer balls. "And that's what counts."

Before the game we practiced kicking the ball into the goal. The first time, Matt tried to do it like a frog, and Lucy tried to stand on the ball. But the second time, they both really kicked it. Matt's shot hit the goalpost. Lucy's went into the net.

"Nice shot, Lucy!" Brenda said. Lucy looked pleased.

Only Alex couldn't come close to a goal. He fell down a lot. And when he didn't fall, he didn't kick it very far. Poor Alex. I felt really bad for him.

"Try once more, Alex," Mom said.

Alex looked sadder than ever. "Okay, Mrs. Antler," he said. "But I don't think it will work!"

Mom rolled the ball to him as gently as she could. Alex pulled his foot way back—and tripped over the ball.

Down he went.

"Are you okay?" Moving like a robot, Mitchell helped him up.

"Mrs. Antler, I have an idea." Brenda's eyes sparkled. "Let's make Alex goalie!" She bounced up and down and grinned. "He's always getting in the way of the ball, right?"

"Right," Mom said slowly.

"Well, the goalie is *supposed* to get in the way of the ball," Brenda said. "So Alex should be goalie."

"That's a great idea!" Josh said.

"Hey, yeah!" Mitchell cried. He took off his shoe. "I bet everybody in the next galaxy thinks it's a good idea, too."

Alex grinned a little and dusted off his pants. "I don't know," he said. "I never played goalie before."

"So what?" Brenda said. "Maybe you'll like it."

Mom smiled and looked at Mitchell. "What do the aliens say?" she asked him.

Mitchell shook his head and frowned

at his shoe. "Nothing, Mrs. Antler," he told her. "They've all gone to bed or something."

"Then I guess I'll have to decide," Mom said. "Alex, you be goalie."

We formed a circle and put our hands together in the middle. "Go, Rangers!" Mom yelled.

"Go, Rangers!" we all yelled back.

Go Rangers!!

Right away a Pirate kicked the ball in my direction. It was coming pretty fast, but I ran up to it anyway.

"Kick it, Catherine!" Matt shouted.

I kicked it as hard as I could.

"Nice play!" yelled Alex.

I patted myself on the back.

A little later another Pirate player was dribbling the ball. He got past Julie. He got past Josh. Then he got past me.

He kicked the ball toward Alex—

But Alex didn't duck. The ball hit his chest and bounced away.

"Great save, Alex!" Lucy cheered.

At halftime the score was tied, 2–2. We all ate apple slices. Lucy didn't try to stand on her ball. And even Matt was listening when Mom told us we were playing well.

With one minute left in the game, each team had three goals. Mitchell had scored twice. Brenda had scored once. It looked as if it would be a tie.

But the best Pirate player had the ball. And she was heading straight for Adam!

"Get it, Adam!" Alex yelled.

I held my breath. Adam didn't run away. He squeezed his knees together.

The girl kicked the ball hard.

"Oof!" Adam grunted. The ball hit his shin guards and rolled away. Adam pumped his fist in the air.

"Nice play, Adam!" I cheered.

But the ball was rolling right to another Pirate player. "Alex!" I yelled.

Quickly Alex dived. Or maybe he just tripped. He reached out—

And knocked the ball away!

"All right!" I yelled.

Brenda passed the ball forward with a good hard kick. I could see it going up in the air, higher and higher. She was passing it to me!

The problem was, the kick was too high. I couldn't get my foot up there. So I stepped back, hoping a Pirate wouldn't get it instead.

"Catherine!" Mom was shouting. "Use your head!"

My head?

My head!

The ball was coming right at me. I had two choices. I could duck, or—

I closed my eyes and leaned sideways. I felt the ball bounce off my head. It didn't even hurt!

"Yay!" Brenda cheered. I could hear her yelling from the other end of the field. "Yay, Catherine!"

I opened my eyes. The ball had bounced to Josh. "Score a goal, Josh!" I shouted. But three Pirates were blocking him.

Josh put his foot on the ball. "Matt!" he yelled.

"Huh?" Matt looked up. His eyes grew big as Josh passed him the ball.

"Kick it, Matt!" I shouted. I was afraid he would pretend to be a frog instead. "Kick it hard!"

Matt pulled his leg back.

"Kick!" I couldn't stand to watch.

Slowly Matt swung his foot forward. This time he didn't kick the grass. The ball rolled toward the goal. The Pirate goalie dived—and missed.

"Goal!" Matt threw his arms into the air. We had won, 4–3!

After the game we ate chocolate bars.

"You guys really played great," Mitchell said. "Even if some of you never played soccer before. Even the aliens think so."

"We sure did." Matt stuck out his chest. "See, Mrs. Antler?" he said proudly. "I did score a real goal, just like you said I would."

Lucy licked her fingers. They were covered with chocolate. "Next time maybe I'll score a goal, too," she said. "I think I'm kind of getting interested in soccer."

"I'm glad," Mom told her. "It really helps to have good teachers, doesn't it?" She winked at Brenda and Mitchell.

"Well, I can teach people, too," Lucy said. She grabbed a soccer ball. "Anybody want to learn to stand on one of these things?" she asked with a big grin.

But I was barely listening. Instead I looked at Mitchell.

"Mitchell," I said, "do you think I could get shoes like yours?"

Mitchell just smiled.

THE LEFTOVERS #4:

REACH THEIR GOAL!

by Tristan Howard

The Rangers aren't exactly the best soccer team in the league. Okay, so they're not even close. But at least they always have fun! Then the Rangers get a new coach—and all he wants the team to do is WIN, WIN, WIN!

COMING IN OCTOBER!